The Callow Pit Coffer

ALSO BY KEVIN CROSSLEY-HOLLAND
AND MARGARET GORDON
The Green Children

THE CALLOW PIT COFFER

Kevin Crossley-Holland

Illustrated by Margaret Gordon

THE SEABURY PRESS · New York

Second Printing

First American edition 1969
Library of Congress Catalog Card Number: 69-13440
Copyright © 1968 by Kevin Crossley-Holland
Illustrations copyright © 1968 by Macmillan, London

Printed in the United States of America

A short glossary appears at the back of the book.

Kieran's

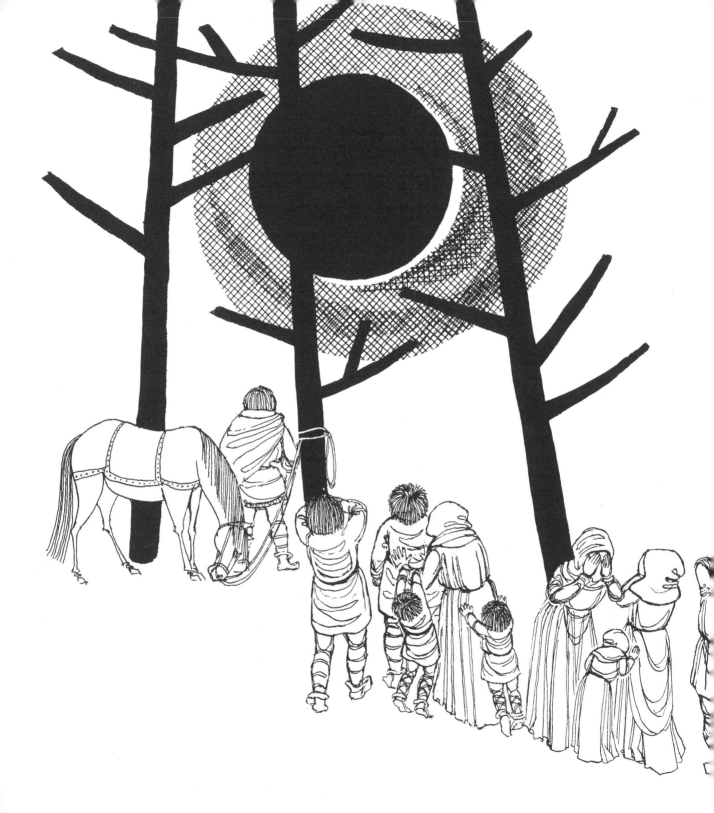

DECEMBER. *Stephen de Blois is King. A cruel month, a cruel time for the people of England. The barons break their oaths to the King, build castles, torture men and women for their gold and silver. And each year it is worse; last March the sun was eclipsed, people trembled and ate their bread by candlelight at noon. "Then corn was dear, and flesh and cheese and butter, for there was none in the land," says the Chronicle. And the Chronicle says: "Never did a country endure greater misery."*

On the estate of one of King Stephen's knights, Sir Jocelin de Neville of Southwood in Norfolk, lies a pool, a pit brimming with dark water. People call it Callow Pit, for the land around is bleak and bare. And they say strange things about it. . . .

7

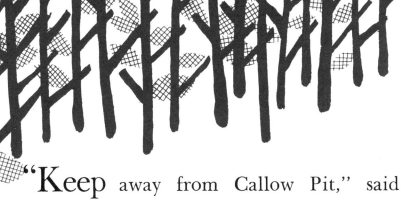

"Keep away from Callow Pit," said
Thor, the old cottar, and he stabbed at the
fire with his stick.

Thor's three sons, Jakke and Keto and the
little cripple Simpkin, had heard his warn-
ing before. They had heard his reasons:
"That place, it's haunted. It's unnatural."
He had told them a hundred times if he had
told them once.

And Simpkin shivered.

But Jakke and Keto glanced at one another; their eyes shifted with some deep
secret only they shared.

Jakke was the elder brother, ill at ease
with other men, a skinflint with words. Yet

he loved animals of every kind, hated to see them suffer the slings of winter; and he was always gentle with Simpkin.

Keto was the rogue everyone liked, the practical joker, the poacher who pinched Sir Jocelin's rabbits and hares and, best of all, his fleet deer; he was red-haired as a fox.

But Jakke and Keto had things in common too: they were both big men, fine wrestlers; they were both brave; danger excited them.

Danger—that was Thor's theme. "There are spirits and phantoms at Callow Pit," he said. "And that's where the headless horseman rides." He jabbed again at the fire. "If you have to pass it, keep your mouths shut. Remember the saying, *If you don't bother them with words, they won't bother you.*"

Callow Pit lay under the shadow of a bald hill, in a gloomy hollow where four ways met. One day the water rose high, the next it sank mysteriously low.

The stories about it, even the sight of it terrified Thor and almost all the other people of Southwood. If you peered into the water, it was so dark you could not see your own face.

"Face to face to face to face, you only give, I only take," warbled the simpleton, Odda. But no one listened to him, neither Thor and his sons, nor anyone else; perhaps he was wiser than they knew.

"I *saw* the headless horseman," whispered Edmund the young cottar to his new wife Emma, new to him, new to the hamlet. "I saw him as he galloped up from the Spon. He rides past Southwood church, skirting

the graveyard, on and on, then disappears near Callow Pit."

"You're shivering, Edmund," said Emma, and wound her arms about him.

Everyone knew Callow Pit was evil. Its black eye watched the world, unblinking. The two oak trees beside it had been struck by lightning, and withered and died.

But everyone in Southwood knew another thing.

"Gold," said Thor, "at the bottom of the

pit." He leaned forward on his stick, nodding his grizzled head, and confided, "In an iron coffer, gold and silver."

"Like the sun and the moon," sighed Simpkin.

"Like your hair," whispered Edmund to Emma, in their hut.

"How did it get there?" said Emma.

"Some people say Danes left it there and never lived to collect it; others that King Edmund concealed it there in case the Danes should get it; and some are sure our grandfathers' fathers hid it when Duke William came. Where did it come from? Nobody knows." Edmund paused. "But God knows we could do with it now, with that devil Sir Jocelin for lord, and the worst of winter still to come."

"Go, then," said Emma. With her blue eyes, she teased him. "If you love me, go and get it."

Edmund stared at her, speechless; a shiver rippled down his spine.

Then Emma burst into laughter, and Edmund laughed too. But he felt disquieted all the same, and wished she had not suggested such a thing, even in jest.

Then they prayed together: "Save us from starving and freezing, O God; O God, give us our daily bread."

And Odda the simpleton, in his hut, said to himself, "Brrr! Poor Odda's heart is gold, but the devil's in him."

Then the north wind blew over the hill and through the hamlet. The freezing blasts carried off everyone's words.

But the very same idea that disquieted Edmund was already at work in the minds of Jakke and Keto. For that was their secret. They were planning to go by night to Callow Pit, and there to fish for gold.

If Thor had known their intention, he would have stiffened with terror and tried to stop them, and sworn by St. William of Norwich that no good would come of it.

"This story, that story about Callow Pit!" said Jakke contemptuously. "I don't believe in them. Old men's chatter! Old wives' tales!" His eyes were the color of iron. "If there's gold, I must get it. Think! Think of all we could do with it! We could walk to Norwich fair, buy horses there, ride home laden with salted meat and corn—"

"If you go, I go," interrupted Keto. His

scalp tingled at the idea, for he half believed the stories himself. But the danger only made him all the more eager. "There'd be enough," he exclaimed, "enough for us, for father and Simpkin, for everyone in South-wood!"

"All right," Jakke agreed. "The two of us."

"When shall we go?" asked Keto.

"As soon as possible," Jakke replied. "By night, when nobody's about. Tomorrow night."

And so they put their heads together and laid their plans, down to the smallest detail.

"There's one last thing," said Keto.

Jakke lifted his eyebrows.

"Those stories. You know those stories?"

Jakke snorted.

As soon as they were sure that Thor and Simpkin were asleep, Jakke and Keto crept out of the smoky hut. Icy fingers of air burned through their clothing.

"Listen," whispered Jakke.

In his own hut, Odda was singing softly: "Beware, I'm an eye, I see you coming. I'll be silent, I'll say nothing. Please say nothing, heal me, heal me, heal me." And his voice was pure as the single bird which defied the darkness and the cold, and cheeped from its perch in the alder tree.

Jakke cocked his head on one side, listening.

"Come on," Keto whispered urgently. "We haven't got all night."

"We have," said Jakke.

Then the brothers stole away from Southwood under the stars and the bruised moon.

They hurried past the hut where Edmund and Emma lay asleep, strode across the common land and round the two open fields, toward the manor of Sir Jocelin de Neville.

With them they brought a long leather thong, and an oak staff with an iron hook. Now they needed Sir Jocelin's ladders.

The manor walls were darker than the darkness. Jakke and Keto stepped through the great gateway and across the deserted courtyard. Their boots crunched on the gravel.

Jakke gritted his teeth. "Quick!"

"There!" said Keto.

They sprang across the yard and snatched the ladders from beneath the haylofts.

"Come on!" urged Jakke.

At once he and Keto hoisted the ladders between them, one on either shoulder.

But Sir Jocelin's wolfhounds, tethered in their kennels, had heard them. They opened their fanged jaws and barked ferociously.

The two brothers, carrying the ladders between them, loped awkwardly across the yard and under the gateway arch once more.

The sound of the barking receded; darkness received them.

"Goodness!" gasped Keto. "Better the devil himself than Sir Jocelin's wolfhounds."

Then, after regaining their breath, they set off once more and, falling into step, strode toward the crossways, and Callow Pit.

"Well!" said Jakke as they approached the pit. "Are you ready?"

Keto nodded.

"Good," said Jakke. "And remember—"

"What was that?" said Keto, stiffening. The nape of his neck tingled.

Jakke stood motionless, listening. "What?" he said. "I didn't hear anything."

"Hooves," replied Keto. "The drumming of hooves."

"I heard nothing," said Jakke.

A small, buffeting wind had got up, a night wind from nowhere, and with it a few clouds that scudded before the moon. It was darker than it was before.

"I said we hadn't got all night," whispered Keto.

Jakke scowled, and put two fingers to his lips. "Remember," he said in a low voice. "Quiet now."

So they came to the hollow where four ways met. The first way led to Southwood, the second to the sea, the third lost itself in a thicket, and the fourth plunged through a cutting where people swore that demons lived.

The bald back of the hill sheltered Callow Pit. The water was still. It was black. It looked like pitch. The gray torsos of the blasted oaks leaned over it.

Jakke and Keto stared down at the pool, then stared at each other. Now they were filled with doubts, and all the stories about Callow Pit crowded into their minds; this

was their moment of going forward, or of turning back.

Jakke went forward, and Keto followed him. He had to, for he was carrying the other end of the ladders. They knelt at the pit's edge and, putting the ladders end to end, bound them tightly together with the leather thong.

Then Jakke motioned to Keto to hold one end and, grasping the other, stepped cautiously round the pool. At last, he stood opposite. Each lowered his end onto the damp earth; they had bridged Callow Pit.

Now Keto, carrying the staff, joined Jakke on the other side. The two brothers peered into the pool; there was no going back now.

Keto handed the staff to Jakke, who, without hesitation, bravely stepped out, a rung at a time, over Callow Pit. One rung, two

rungs, three rungs, four rungs. Five rungs—
the bank already looked a long way off.

Keto, like a henchman, followed two
rungs behind him.

The ladders held firm. They were stout,
and strongly bound.

A third of the way across the pit, Jakke
glanced over his shoulder; Keto nodded. So
he grasped the staff more firmly; his knuckles
gleamed like ivory. Then he drew in his
breath and plunged the hook into the water.

A raven screeched, starting from its hide-
out in the oak stump.

Jakke leaned forward and prodded the
bottom of the pit. And Keto watched anx-
iously.

Jakke straightened, shook his head, drew
the dripping staff out of the water and turned
about. Then he plunged it in a second time.

The result was just the same.

So the two brothers stepped forward again until Keto stood in the very middle of the pit. His blood whirled; he felt giddy. He took the staff from Jakke and rammed it into the loathsome water. And if Jakke hadn't grabbed at him, he would have lost his balance entirely.

Be calm, Keto, be careful, Jakke gestured with his hands.

Now Keto sank the iron-hooked staff into the water again.

"*Cluung!*" They heard it directly; the clang of metal against metal, muted by water.

Keto drew in his breath sharply. He went down on one knee and probed more carefully. It *feels* like the coffer, he thought. It's the right shape. It *is* the coffer!

Suddenly, the iron hook was snagged. Keto pulled at the staff; some force had caught against it. He pulled harder, and harder, and the weight began to move.

Then Jakke crouched forward and gripped the staff as well. He tugged with all his strength. The ladders groaned. And slowly, slowly, swaying like drunkards, the two brothers lifted up and out of the water, inch by inch, a dripping, crusted, iron coffer.

They gasped at it: at its weight; at the great lock on it; at the massive ring in its lid which had snagged their hook.

Carefully, they lowered it onto the ladders. And the ladders creaked and complained more angrily, sagged at the center.

Oh, the gold and silver, thought Keto. His mind sang like a bird. Food for us, for Thor and Simpkin, for everyone else . . .

this winter, every winter . . . not one piece for Sir Jocelin. . . .

Jakke tapped Keto on the shoulder and took the staff from him. He slipped it through the ring so they could sling the coffer between them. Then each brother put one end of the staff over his shoulder. The gold seemed light as a load of feathers. They were rich, more than rich; they were ready to go.

Keto was so elated he could have climbed to the moon. The stars in the sky seemed to spray like sparks over him. He tossed his head and shouted gaily: "We've got it, we've got it; the devil himself can't get it from us now!"

At once a yellowish mist surged up from the water, and swirled angrily about them. It caught at their throats; they coughed and spluttered and choked.

Birds shrieked out of the stillness of
night; the air was full of the flapping of
wings. Wolves howled. Grass blades stiffened. The hackles of all natural things rose
at the unnatural.

"Quick!" yelled Jakke. "Quick, Keto!"

It was too late. Out of the water thrust a
hideous black hand, then a huge black arm.

Jakke and Keto curdled with terror.

They recoiled. A step further, and they would have toppled backward into the pit.

The unearthly hand clawed at the ladder; its nails were like spikes.

Keto bared his teeth. "Don't let go," he growled, terrified, yet furiously determined not to lose the coffer.

Jakke responded. He crushed his end of the staff in his grip.

Face to face with the powers of darkness, Jakke and Keto found strength in themselves; they pulled like demons.

The ladders groaned and curved like a crossbow; cold water gripped their ankles.

Then the arm wound round the coffer, and yanked it.

Jakke and Keto lurched forward onto their toes, rocked back onto their heels.

They refused to let go.

"Pull, pull," urged Keto. "PULL!"

The yellow vapor wrapped them in its hundred arms; the oak staff stood firm, stronger than them all.

They pulled again, with the strength of ten men. Then metal screamed; the coffer and the ring in its lid were torn apart.

At one and the same moment, three things happened: the ladders separated under the tremendous strain; Jakke and Keto cried out as they fell backward into the water; and the coffer, the coffer hit the surface of the pool with a colossal splash. It disappeared from sight.

The two brothers wrestled with the black,

heaving water; at last they waded to the bank together.

Sodden and shivering, still in possession of the staff and the ring, Jakke and Keto sat on the damp earth, a little way off from the pit.

For what seemed like a long time, neither of them spoke. Fowls returned to their perches; wolves no longer howled. Already

the cold green light of dawn showed in the east.

At last, Jakke broke the silence. All he said was, "Keto, Keto."

And Keto shook his head dumbly.

So the coffer they had not, because Keto had forgotten the saying, and spoken words; but they had the ring for their pains—the massive iron ring as a proof of their exploit.

Jakke and Keto looked at and fingered it, wonderingly.

Yellow tinged the pale green of the east; all was not lost even if the coffer was lost.

Jakke stood up and stretched. "We should go now," he said.

"The ladders," said Keto in a small voice. His arms ached so much that he didn't know how he would be able to carry them back to the manor.

"Confound the ladders!" said Jakke.

So the two brothers took the way to South-wood; and presently the lead melted out of their feet, and they swung their arms. They began to talk about what had happened, and especially about the black hand; the thought of it, huge and hideous in their minds, was worse even than the sight of it.

Keto cursed his wagging tongue that had cost them the gold. "I'm sorry, Jakke," he said, simply and humbly.

Jakke turned to him. *"If you don't bother them . . ."* he said. And he was scowling and grinning at one and the same time.

"Where have you been?" demanded Thor angrily as soon as Jakke and Keto stepped into the hut. He saw they were haggard and soaked to the skin. He glared at them under his thunderous brows. "Where have you been? What's that ring?"

"We'll tell you," said Keto.

"You will," said Thor. "I'm still your father, aren't I? Where have you been?"

"Callow Pit," said Jakke.

"Where?" exploded Thor. He didn't believe them; he didn't want to believe them.

"Callow Pit," repeated Jakke, as if he had just been in Edmund's hut.

And Simpkin, sitting in the corner, flaxen-haired, stared up at his brothers as if they were ghosts.

"You see this ring?" said Keto, lifting it between his hands like a crown.

"What is it?" muttered Thor uneasily.

So, sodden and exhausted as they were,

Jakke and Keto told them the whole story, from first to last. Its telling was punctuated by many questions and exclamations. And Thor, who had begun by being angry and fearful, ended by being fearful and proud.

Simpkin, too, glowed with pride at the daring of his brothers. But there was an ache in his heart because he had not gone with them, because he had never shared their adventures and never would. It was not envy now, though once it had been so; it was simply a sadness to be endured.

Then Thor hurried out into the sharp, early morning air. Thin streams of smoke rose from each hut. He was full of the story, anxious to tell anyone and everyone, and as quickly as he could.

He was not disappointed. In all his life, he had never been paid so much attention.

In the two fields that day, and over food, and in the smoky firelight, Jakke and Keto and Callow Pit were the only topic of conversation.

Edmund and Emma listened to the story standing shoulder to shoulder; and as it unfolded, their eyes opened wider and wider. Then Edmund remembered how Emma had dared him to go to Callow Pit; he felt uneasy once more, and almost a

coward, and envied Jakke and Keto even as he praised them for their great bravery.

But Emma, she trembled at the thought of how Edmund might have taken her seriously, and gone to Callow Pit. And now she wished, as Edmund had wished before, that she had not suggested such a thing at all, even in fun.

But then their eyes met; and, as always, they soon forgot everything, even the story, except one another.

When the tale was told in the hearing of Odda, he sat bolt upright and listened most attentively: and later he was heard to say, sagely, sadly: "I am what I was, alas, alas. Dark's still in me; dispossess me."

"What shall we do with the ring?" said Keto.

"I'm not having it in here," said Thor at

AUTHOR'S NOTE

The story of the Callow Pit Coffer was written down by John Glyde in *The Norfolk Garland* (1872); I have been unable to find an earlier source than that. But this tale is age old (I have chosen to set it in the reign of King Stephen), and such motifs as the headless horseman, the crossroads, and the presence of the powers of darkness recur from the earliest times in the folk tales of Great Britain.

Southwood lies between Norwich and Yarmouth. It is a bleak hamlet, surrounded by boggy land. A disastrous flood, then a virulent plague, swept through it in 1606, killing many inhabitants; since then, its population has steadily decreased, and today only two or three families remain there. People do not move to Southwood; they only move away from it.

When the Church of St. Edmund at Southwood (it was a thatched church) fell into disrepair in 1881, the iron ring from Callow Pit was taken to the neighboring parish of Limpenhoe and fastened to the Church door. It is there now.

GLOSSARY

the Chronicle: The Anglo-Saxon Chronicle, a year by year history of England inspired by King Alfred and continued up to 1154, the end of the reign of King Stephen.

cottar: a peasant, a cottager who owned an acre or two of his own but had to do a certain amount of work on his lord's land.

Edmund: a ninth-century King of the East Anglians, who was killed by the Danes in 869.

open fields: the arable land of an ordinary village, cultivated in two great open fields which were divided into strips belonging to the cottars and their lord.

Southwood: it lies several miles to the south of the Norwich–Yarmouth road; the nearest town is Acle.

the Spon: a boggy place.

Stephen de Blois: King of England, 1135–1154.

sulphurous mist: traditionally regarded as hellish.